1984

University of St. Francis
GEN 869.3 A481sm
Amado, Jorge,
The swallow and the tom cat :

3 0301 00090866 1

A GOOD PLACE TO LIVE IN
THIS WORLD WOULD BE
IF THE DAY SHOULD HAPPEN
WHERE ONE COULD SEE
A SWALLOW MARRY
A STRIPED CAT
AND IF THOSE TWO
COULD FLY AWAY—
HAPPY TOGETHER
FOREVER AND A DAY

(Verse and philosophy of Estêvão da Escuna,
popular poet at the Market of Seven Gates in Bahia)

THE

TRANSLATED BY BARBARA SHELBY MERELLO

DESIGNED BY JOAN STOLIAR WITH
ILLUSTRATIONS BY CARYBÉ

DELACORTE⊕PRESS/ELEANOR FRIEDE

JORGE AMADO

SWALLOW AND THE TOM CAT

A LOVE STORY

LIBRARY
College of St. Francis
JOLIET, ILL.

OTHER BOOKS BY JORGE AMADO:

HOME IS THE SAILOR

TIETA

DONA FLOR AND HER TWO HUSBANDS

GABRIELA, CLOVE AND CINNAMON

SHEPHERDS OF THE NIGHT

TENT OF MIRACLES

TEREZA BATISTA: HOME FROM THE WARS

THE TWO DEATHS OF QUINCAS WATERYELL

THE VIOLENT LAND

Published by
Delacorte Press / Eleanor Friede
1 Dag Hammarskjold Plaza
New York, N.Y. 10017

This work was originally published in Brazil as O GATO MALHADO
E A ANDORINHA SINHÁ:UMA HISTORIA DE AMOR by Distribuidora
Record. Copyright © 1976 by Jorge Amado.

Translation copyright © 1982 by Dell Publishing Co., Inc., and
Distribuidora Record

Design copyright © 1982 by Joan Stoliar

All rights reserved. No part of this book may be reproduced or
transmitted in any form or by any means, electronic or
mechanical, including photocopying, recording, or by any
information storage and retrieval system, without the written
permission of the Publisher, except where permitted by law.

Manufactured in the United States of America

Designed by Joan Stoliar

Library of Congress Cataloging in Publication Data
Amado, Jorge, 1912–
    The swallow and the tom cat.
    Translation of: O gato malhado e a andorinha
Sinhá.
    I. Title
PS9697.A647G3813 1982 869'.3 82-10038
ISBN 0-440-08325-7

869.3
Q481am

12-29-83   Almond $5.59

THIS IS A TALE OF ONCE UPON
A TIME IN THE DIM FORGOTTEN
DAYS WHEN ANIMALS COULD
TALK, WHEN DOG LEASHES
WERE MADE OF SAUSAGES,
WHEN TAILORS MARRIED
PRINCESSES, AND CHILDREN
WERE BROUGHT INTO THE
WORLD BY STORKS.
BOYS AND GIRLS NOWADAYS
ARE BORN KNOWING ALL
THERE IS TO KNOW;
THEY HAVE THEMSELVES
ANALYZED BEFORE THEY'RE
BORN SO THAT EACH CHILD
CAN PICK HIS FAVORITE
COMPLEX: ANXIETY, LONELINESS,
VIOLENCE. MY LOVE STORY
HAPPENED LONG, LONG AGO
WHEN THINGS WERE DIFFERENT.

108, 186

DAWN

Here comes Morning, slow and sleepy, three quarters of an hour late on the job as usual. She can hardly muster up the energy to open her eyes as she trails her lazy way among the clouds. Oh, how she wishes she could just sleep on and on with no alarm clock to wake her up, sleep until she isn't sleepy any more! The day she catches herself a rich husband will be the last day Morning ever opens her eyes before eleven, if then. Curtains on the windows so the light won't get in her eyes, breakfast in bed . . . the innocent dreams of a marriageable girl. Real life for a junior civil servant on a strict schedule is quite a different story. It's up before dawn to put out the stars that Night always turns on because she's afraid of the dark. Night's scared of her own shadow.

Morning puts out each star with a kiss as she trails her leisurely way toward the horizon. Yawning and half-asleep, she's bound to miss a few, and then the poor stars have to twinkle on all day, trying their best to shine. Then comes the really hard job: warming up the Sun, a task for giants and not for a dainty young thing like her. She has to coax the dying embers from the day before into a first feeble spark and then nurse it into flame. It would take Morning hours to light the Sun if she had to do it by herself. But the Wind, notorious blowhard that he is, almost always comes to her aid. Why does that silly fellow insist he was just passing by when everybody knows he really happens along accidentally on purpose? Is there anybody who hasn't heard about the Wind's secret passion for Morning? Secret? It's the talk of the whole wide world!

A lot of malicious gossip about the Wind is making the rounds. People say he's a rogue, a rake and a braggart—a ne'er-do-well and no model for anyone. They talk about his crazy tricks: blowing out lights, lanterns, lamps, and candles to frighten poor Night half to death, and stripping the trees of their lovely, leafy drapery to leave them with nothing on at all. Practical jokes in the worst of taste; and yet, incredible as it may seem, Night heaves a sigh when he comes near and the trees in the wood, shameless creatures, shiver with delight when he goes by.

The Wind's favorite joke is slipping under women's skirts and lifting them up with the worst of intentions. This trick never failed to draw a crowd in the old days; you should have heard the laughter, the sly sidelong glances, the smothered exclamations, the hearty *Ohs!* and *Ahs!* But that was in the good old days. Nowadays the Wind has no success at all when he tries to show off that stale old trick. What is there left to show, now that everything is on show all the time and the more we see, the less we want to see it? You never can tell, of course; maybe future generations will turn against the easy and the obvious. Maybe they'll start picketing and demonstrating and clamoring for what's hidden and hard to get.

The Wind is more than a little crazy, and it's no use denying he has his faults. But why not speak up for his undeniable virtues, too? After all he's cheerful, light-hearted, and light-footed, the best dancing partner in the world and a good comrade, too, who's always ready to help a friend, especially a lady, young or old.

No matter how early, no matter how cold, wherever he is and however rough and distant the road, faithfully at dawn the Wind comes to the house of the Sun to help little Morning. He puffs with might and main, his great mouth full of air. Yet no sooner have the coals leapt into flame than he leaves the task of fanning the fire to Morning and settles down to reminisce about the adventures he's had and the things he's seen in his wanderings over the earth: snowy mountaintops far above the clouds and chasms so deep that Morning could never hope to see the bottom.

Boastful, reckless, a vagabond king crossing borders, invading empty spaces and scouring hidden places, the Wind carries a sackful of tales for whoever wants to listen and learn.

And since Morning never can resist the lure of a good story, she falls even further behind schedule as she listens enthralled to the Wind spinning his tales, sad or gay, some of them so long they have to be told a chapter at a time. Never one to work any harder than she has to, Morning lets herself be carried away, now smiling, now pensive, now bursting into tears—after all, the best stories are the ones that make you cry. Small wonder the clocks go wild. They have no choice but to slow down their hands and pendulums, marking time until Morning appears and they can strike the hour of five. Many a clock and watch has gone quite mad and never kept the right time since—always slow or fast—turning day into night. Others have simply stopped, once and for all. A certain celebrated clock in the tower of the celebrated factory that turns out those celebrated watches that keep the most accurate time in the world, itself the Olympic champion of meticulous timepieces, actually committed suicide by hanging itself from its own hour and minute hands when Morning's perpetual tardiness became too much for it. It was a Swiss watch with an extraordinary sense of responsibility and boundless loyalty to the firm.

It wasn't just the clocks, either. Roosters lost their heads, crowing at the wrong time, heralding the Sun long before Morning, distracted by the Wind's tales, had gotten around to lighting it. Such cocks became permanently crestfallen. So clocks and cocks stormed off to Time, the lord of them

14

all, with a list of eight accusations and twenty-six unanswerable arguments. Time was not much impressed, however. Why bother about an hour here, an hour there, when all eternity stretched out ahead? A broken rule now and then varied the monotony, at least, and besides, Time never troubled to conceal a certain weakness for Morning. Blithe and inconsequential as she was, young and silly and averse to rules and regulations, she had the power to make him forget, for a while, the weary weight of eternity, along with his chronic bronchitis.

One day, though, the forgetful creature really went too far. The Wind had wanted to break up one of his long tales into two or three installments in the telling, but she insisted on hearing the whole story, complete with every detail, from beginning to end. And by the time they separated, the Sun should long since have been blazing high in the sky.

Dressed in white light sprinkled with blue and crimson flowers, Morning drifted absentmindedly through the clouds, still thinking about the tale the Wind had told her. Dreamily she recalled one detail after another, feeling a pleasant twinge of melancholy as she did so. A learned author might describe her sentiments as mixed.

She would have liked to be somebody else instead of Morning with her strict obligations, so that she could lie down in the fields at dawn and think about the Wind's

15

intentions. Why had he picked that particular story? Just because he liked it? Morning suspected another reason, some secret intention hinted at in the Wind's half-closed eyes and an unexpected sigh at the climax of the tale.

Did the Wind sigh for her; was the whispered gossip true? Did he really intend to ask for her hand in marriage? Marrying the Wind wasn't such a bad idea, though Morning would have preferred a millionaire. The Wind could help her blow out the stars, light the Sun, dry the dew and open the flower nicknamed Eleven-o'clock, which Morning, just to be contrary, opened every day between nine-thirty and ten. If she married the Wind, she could roam the world at her husband's side, fly over the highest ranges, ski down the eternal snow-slopes, run lightly over the sea's green back, play leapfrog with the waves and rest when she was tired in one of the underground caves where darkness hides in the daytime to go to sleep.

But was the Wind, that fickle, fancy-free old bachelor, thinking seriously of marrying and settling down? He had played a leading part in dozens of romantic adventures, scandals and love affairs. She had heard stories of abductions and pursuits, jealous husbands, vows of vengeance. Morning shook her head. No, marriage was probably the last thing the Wind had in mind; his intentions were not so innocent. In less modern times, they would have been called strictly dishonorable.

There was no harm in dreaming, even so. Absorbed in a reverie of pleasant thoughts, Morning dawdled on her way and forgot the time. Every clock was stopped and waiting; all the roosters were hoarse from crowing for a sun that wouldn't rise. What had happened to the sun? People roused by the frantic noise glanced at the time, saw that it was five o'clock, then realized there was no sun. The feeble light of dawn struggled in the folds of Night's gray, gauzy train. Was this the end of the world? It certainly looked that way.

In the face of such flagrant tardiness and so many complaints, Time felt obliged to give Morning a stern talking-to, although he had to conceal a smile on his solemn, bearded, wrinkled face the whole time he was scolding her and threatening to punish her. Morning piped up in her birdlike treble and confessed the truth.

"The Wind was telling me such a good story, Father, that I forgot the time."

"A story?" Time pricked up his ears, always interested in anything that might lighten the tedious weight of eternity. "Suppose you tell it to me, and if it's really good, I'll not only forgive you, I'll give you a blue rose that used to flourish centuries ago but is no longer to be found. For everything has changed, my child, and changed for the worse. Nothing is the way it used to be, and all the best things in life have vanished, alas." Time is always yearning for the past.

Morning sat down at the feet of the Master with a flounce of her luminous skirts and began her tale. Time dozed off before she was halfway through, but Morning went right on. As the story unfolded she seemed to hear the caressing voice of the Wind and see the pleading look in his bold eyes. "Where are you, restless, vagabond Wind?" she wondered. In what corner of the world was he, peering slyly at what he shouldn't see, stripping trees, penetrating clouds, pursuing the Rain as she fled through the sky and finally flinging her down on the green grass? They were intimate friends, Wind and Rain, too intimate—and accomplices in mischief. Or were they more than that? Suddenly troubled, Morning frowned.

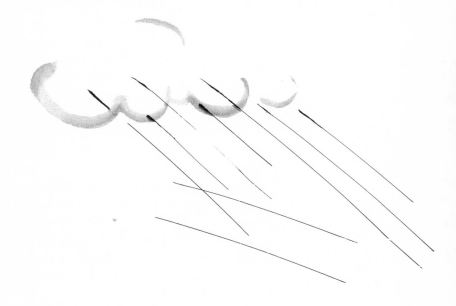

Parenthetical Remark

(The story that Morning told Time to win the blue rose was the tale of Miss Swallow and the Striped Tom Cat, told her by the Wind in a plaintive murmur interspersed with sighs. I've written it down just as I heard it from Dr. Cururu, the illustrious Toad who lives on top of a mossy stone by a marshy pond in a wild and desolate place. This eminent Toad, an old crony of the Wind, told me about the affair as proof of his friend's lack of seriousness. In the Toad's opinion the Wind was wasting his time spinning fantasies when he could have been turning the experience gained on his travels to advantage by studying some worthwhile subject like communications, Sanskrit, or acupuncture. Dr. Cururu has his Ph.D., of course, and is a professor of linguistics and body language, an expert on Rock, a full, corresponding or honorary member of a number of learned societies here and abroad, and fluent in several dead languages. If the beauty of this story doesn't move you, don't blame the Wind or Morning, much less the sage Toad, Doctor Honoris Causa. No story told in human speech can hope to preserve the purity and charm of the original; the poetry and music of the Wind are lost.)

SPRING

When Spring came back into the world dressed in light and gorgeous colors and scented with subtle perfumes, unfurling blossoms and dressing the trees in leaf green, the Cat stretched his legs and opened his mean, dun-colored eyes. Everyone who knew him thought he had mean, ugly eyes. In fact, they said the Tom Cat's evil nature showed not only in his eyes but in his whole strong, agile, yellow and black striped body. He was a middle-aged cat who had long outgrown his first youth and had almost forgotten the days when he loved to scamper through the woods and prowl on the rooftops, yowling depraved love songs at the moon. No one could imagine him ever singing anything romantic.

There was no more selfish, solitary creature to be found for miles around. The Cat was not on friendly terms with his neighbors and he almost never responded to the rare greeting mumbled by some polite or fearful passerby. He would snarl and close his eyes as if disgusted by the spectacle around him.

And yet, the life being lived quietly or noisily around him was a fine sight to see. Perfumed buds blossomed out into radiant flowers, gaily trilling birds fluttered or soared, pigeons cooed lovingly, broods of

21

newborn chicks followed their proud, cackling mothers, Black Duck courted White Duck, bathing with her in the clear, calm waters of the lake, and frolicsome puppies gamboled, leaped and rolled on the grass.

As for the Tom Cat, nobody went near him. The flowers closed their petals when he came prowling around; they said that he had knocked over, with a swipe of his paw, a shy white lily that all the roses had been in love with. There was no real proof he had done it, but who could doubt that the big cat was a bully? Birds flew higher when they passed over the place where he slept. People even whispered that it had been the wicked Striped Cat who had stolen Sabia, the baby thrush, out of his nest of twigs. When Mother Sabia flew back bringing food and found her nestling gone, she had ended her life by pressing her soft breast up against the thorns of a night-blooming cereus. The funeral was a sad one and many a curse was flung at the Cat that day. There was no proof of his guilt, but who else could have done it? All you had to do was look at the beast's face to know he was the murderer. Yes, he was an ugly critter and no mistake.

The pigeons flew a long way off to nestle and coo. They were practically certain it was the Cat who had killed and eaten the prettiest turtledove in the dovecote, and since then all the joy had gone out of a certain carrier pigeon's life. Again, there was no proof, but as the Reverend Parrot said, "Who could have committed such a crime but that evil rogue who feared neither God nor the Law?"

The mother hens taught their yellow chicks how to avoid the Striped Cat, in whose criminal clutches, so they affirmed, many other chicks had perished, not to mention the eggs he stole out of nests to feed his ignoble fat self. Black Duck stayed clear of him altogether, for the big cat had no liking at all for the lake in which the pair of ducks were in their element. As for the puppies, when they tried to coax him to run and jump with them he had clawed their little muzzles, bristled the hair on his back and insulted their family, their breed, and several generations of their ancestors.

Yes, he was a wicked, selfish cat, a bad cat through and through. In the morning he would lie down on the grass to sun himself, but no sooner did the Sun rise in the sky than he would leave it and stalk away in search of cool shade. Ungrateful was the word for him. For quite some time a Guava Tree with a gnarled trunk was under the delusion that the Tom Cat was in love with her because he would steal up to her with agile, sensual grace and rub up against her

knotty trunk on long sunny afternoons, and she boasted of it to all the other trees in the park. That Guava Tree, who was known as something of a character herself, felt flattered that such a difficult, controversial fellow should show a partiality for her. She consulted a plastic surgeon, who carefully removed all the ugly knots from her trunk to make her beautiful for the Striped Cat, and then she stood in her pretty, smooth new bark and waited. When the Cat saw there were no more knots and hollows on that trunk to scratch himself on, he turned his back on the Guava and never even looked at her again. Everyone in the park made fun of the Guava for a long time afterward because of that episode. Even Old Owl, who lived in the Jackfruit Tree, laughed when she heard about it.

In all fairness I must admit that the Tom Cat was ignorant of his own bad reputation. If he knew, he didn't care. After all, he hardly said a word to any of them except occasionally to Owl. It was true that Owl, whose opinion counted for something because of her age, always said the Tom Cat couldn't be as bad as he was painted and

that the others might be mistaken about him. They listened, shook their heads, and despite their respect for Owl, continued to give the Cat a wide berth.

And so time passed until Spring danced into the park in a whirl of color, fragrance and song. Bright colors, dizzying fragrance, resounding song. The Tom Cat was asleep when Spring burst forth in all her glory. So strong and insistent was her call that the Cat started from his dreamless sleep, opened his yellow-brown eyes and stretched his limbs. Black Duck, who happened to be looking at him, almost fell over with amazement. He could have sworn the Striped Tom was smiling. He stared and then nudged White Duck.

"Is he laughing or isn't he?"

"Good Lord! He *is!*"

No one had ever seen him laugh. The little White Duck was so startled by the chuckle that came out of the Tom Cat's fierce throat that she put her hand to her heart. There was laughter on his lips and what was even more astonishing, laughter in his yellow eyes as well.

All at once he rolled over on the grass like a crazy young tom cat and let out a meow that was almost a moan. What a commotion in the park! The Speckled Hen, passing by with her golden brood, cried out "Oh, my land!" and fainted on top of her chicks.

25

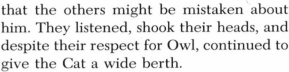

108, 186

LIBRARY
College of St. Francis
JOLIET, ILL.

Don Juan of Rhode Island, the Rooster, came running up to see what had happened to the Speckled Hen, his favorite of all the ladies in his harem. He helped her up and was about to launch into his clarion war call when the Striped Cat rolled over in the grass again and let out another heartfelt meow. A lovesick meow from that Cat! Impossible!

Don Juan of Rhode Island choked down his challenge to battle, and a deep hush fell over the park just as Spring settled in. Even the pigeons stopped their amorous cooing, so great was the general surprise at the Tom Cat's strange behavior.

"I believe he's lost his mind" was the diagnosis of a Wormseed Bush known for his medical competence.

"He's getting ready to work some new piece of devilment, if you ask me," whispered the Speckled Hen, now recovered from her conniptions, as she led away her chicks and Don Juan of Rhode Island.

Meanwhile the Striped Cat rose to his feet, stretched his limbs, ruffled the fur on his back to feel the full effect of the suddenly welcome warmth of the sun, expanded his nostrils to breathe in the sweet new smells floating in the air around him, relaxed into a broad smile for all the world, and stepped out jauntily into the sunshine.

Pandemonium! The big Black Duck dived to the bottom of the lake, dragging White Duck with him, and broke his own

26

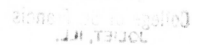

record for underwater swimming as he crossed to the opposite bank and deposited his little wife safely ashore. The pigeons all flocked to the dovecote and there was no more cooing in the branches, where a myriad of green shoots were being transformed into shady leaves almost as fast as they appeared. The dogs stopped running and jumping and pretended to be very busy all of a sudden digging for bones. Flowers stopped budding and one premature rose who had already opened dropped all her petals on the ground but one, which was borne to and fro for a time by the breeze.

All this running about caused something of a stir, and the Tom Cat noticed it and wondered. Why was everyone in such a hurry to leave now, when the park was at its loveliest and Spring had just come? Was a storm coming up? But no, there was no chill wind scattering the leaves, no rain pouring over the rooftops. Why on earth should the animals run away and hide when Spring was here and life was so sweet? Was the Diamondback Rattler here again? Had she dared slink back into the park? The Cat looked around. If it was that no-good snake, he'd have to teach her another lesson, so she'd never dare come back to rob eggs, pull baby birds down out of their nests and gobble up chickens and turtledoves. But the Rattlesnake wasn't there. The Tom Cat thought and thought. Finally it dawned on him that they were

running away from *him*. They hadn't
heard him meow or seen him smile in so
long, they were simply scared out of their
wits.

It was a sad awakening. First his smile
faded, then he shrugged indifferently. He
was a proud cat and didn't much care what
other animals thought of him. He winked a

roguish eye at the Sun, a wink so unexpected that an enormous Stone, which had lived in the same nearby spot for ages, rolled away into the forest.

The Cat breathed in great gulps of new spring air. He felt lightheaded and giddy. He longed to make silly noises, saunter around the park, maybe even talk to somebody. He looked all around with his yellow eyes, but nobody was there. Every single one of them had run away.

All but one. In the branch of a flowering tree Miss Swallow was watching the Striped Cat and smiling at him. She was the only one who hadn't run away. Her parents called out to her nervously from a distance.

The denizens of the park peeked out fearfully from their hiding places as the Swallow smiled at the Tom Cat. And all around them was Spring, a poet's dream.

Another
Parenthetical Aside

TO INTRODUCE MISS SWALLOW

(When she passed by, laughing and full of life, there wasn't a male bird within sight who didn't sigh longingly. She was still very young, of course, but all the lads in the park followed after her wherever she went. They declared their love and wrote poems to her, and the Nightingale, the most famous troubadour of them all, sang beneath her window by moonlight. She had a smile for each and was friendly with all of them, but gave her heart to none. The lively, curious little chatterbox fluttered from tree to tree in the park with all the carefree gaiety of an innocent heart. Everyone agreed that none of the neighboring parks could boast such a sweet beautiful bird as their own Miss Swallow.)

SPRING

Spring was everywhere, the dream of a poet. Tom Cat felt an impulse to say something of the sort to the little Swallow. He sat down on the ground, smoothed his whiskers and asked:

"So you didn't run away like the others?"

"Me, run away? I'm not afraid of you. The others are just a bunch of cowards. You couldn't catch me if you tried; you don't have wings to fly. You're just a bad old silly cat and ugly as sin besides."

"Ugly? Me?"

The Tom Cat let out a frightful laugh that was more like a rusty yowl; he hadn't laughed in so long, and this time even the bravest trees, like the giant Brazilwood, trembled. "She insulted him and now he'll kill her for sure," thought the old Great Dane.

The Reverend Parrot—Reverend because he had lived for a while in a seminary, where he had learned how to pray and had memorized a few Latin phrases, enough to earn him a reputation as a wise old bird—shut his eyes so as not to be a witness to the impending tragedy. He shut them for two reasons: because he was softhearted and hated the thought of seeing blood spilled, especially that of a dear little swallow; and because he had no desire to

be called as a witness if the case were
brought into court. A fine fix he'd be in,
having to choose between telling the truth
and taking the consequences of the Tom
Cat's fury—being slapped with a libel suit,
or knocked down and having his beak torn
off or Lord knows what—or lying in his
teeth and then being reviled as a coward
and an accomplice to murder. It was a hard
choice to make, but it was plainly wiser not
to testify against the Cat. He began praying
very hard for the Swallow's soul to still the
insistent voice of his conscience.

The Swallow herself realized that she
had gone too far. She flew up to a higher
branch, just in case, and began to preen her
feathers in an extremely coquettish fash-
ion. The Cat was still laughing, although he
was really put out, not because the Swallow
had called him bad, but because she
thought him ugly. He thought himself
handsome, a very fine cat indeed, a most
elegant feline.

"Come on, now. You don't really think
I'm ugly?"

"Didn't you hear me say you're as ugly as sin?" the Swallow called out from a safe distance.

"I don't believe you. You'd have to be blind to think I was ugly."

"Ugly and conceited, too!"

The conversation broke off just then because the Swallow's parents, whose love for their child had at last overcome their fear, came flying up and bore her away with them, scolding her all the way home. As she was being carried away the Swallow called back to the Cat, "See you later, my ugly one!"

With this rather idiotic exchange of words the tale of the Tom Cat and the Swallow began.

As far as the Swallow was concerned, it had begun long before that. I should have explained a few things about this young Swallow in an earlier chapter. Since I missed the chance to insert the explanation in its proper place in the narrative, all I can do now is stop the action and backtrack a little. This is a confusing way to tell a story; I realize that. But my lapse of memory can plausibly be blamed on the turmoil stirred up in cats and storytellers by the coming of Spring. Or better yet, I can say I'm revolutionizing narrative form and structure and win instant support from academic critics and literary columnists for saying so.

OPENING CHAPTER

DELAYED AND OUT OF PLACE

Besides being pretty, Miss Swallow was rather headstrong; "unconventional" would be a nicer way of putting it. She was only a young girl, still going to Birds' School where the Parrot taught religion. Although her parents didn't allow her to go out in the evening with birds of the opposite sex, she was decidedly independent and proud to be on good terms with everybody in the park. She made friends with flowers and trees, ducks and hens, dogs and stones and pigeons and the lake. She found something to say to each of them, with a little self-possessed air and no notion of the hearts that beat faster in her presence.

Even the Reverend Parrot, who put on such virtuous airs and was looked up to almost like a man of the cloth because he had lived in a seminary, gazed at her through half-closed eyes during class.

In spite of all her interesting friends and admirers, there was a cloud in the young girl's sky, the reason for this tardy first chapter. The cloud was the Striped Cat, or rather her failure ever to have had a talk with him. The proud, gruff, unsociable animal annoyed her no end. She had fallen into the habit of spying on him as he lay sleeping or sunning himself on the grass. She would watch him from a hidden perch in a tree for hours at a time, at a loss to understand why the ornery beast was so standoffish. Naturally she had heard the bad things that were said about him, but when she looked at his pink nose and long whiskers she wondered—just why, she couldn't have said—whether the stories were true. That's swallows for you; once they start wondering, there simply is no way of making them understand the plainest, most obvious truth. They trust their own judgment and they follow their hearts.

The Tom Cat was the one shadow that lay across Miss Swallow's sunny, peaceful life. Sometimes when she was singing one of the pretty songs the Nightingale had taught her, she would stop right in the middle because she saw, or thought she saw, the bulky form of the Cat going by on his way to his favorite corner. Then she would fly up a little way and flutter along behind him. One afternoon she amused herself for the longest time by throwing dry twigs down on his back. The Cat was asleep and she was invisible among the leaves of the Jack Tree, laughing each time a twig pinged down on the Cat's back and made the lazy creature open one eye and look all around, only to shut it again immediately, thinking it was just the Wind playing one of his silly tricks. The Cat had learned long ago that it was no use running after the Wind and trying to bat him with his paw. It was better just to wait until the Wind got tired of his joke. But this time, since the

teasing didn't stop, he gave up and decided
to go somewhere else where he could rest.
Miss Swallow flew off in great glee at the
joke she had played on the Tom Cat that
everybody else was so afraid of.

On that same day she had a famous conversation with the Solemn Cow. I'm intro-
ducing the Solemn Cow in the first chapter
of my book because she was one of the most
important people in the park and was
looked up to almost as much as Old Owl.
This cow was descended from an Argentine
bull and her name was Rachel Pucio. She
was a sedate, rather formal person, highly
respectable and extremely circumspect.
On the other hand, she had an unforgiving
nature and uneven temper. The soul of
kindness to those she was fond of—Mr. and
Mrs. Duck, for instance, were great friends
of hers—she could be rude and vengeful
toward anyone who offended her: the
Horsefly, all dogs, and most especially the
Striped Cat.

The Cow had an old grudge against the
Tom Cat. She considered that her highly
respectable person, Argentine blood and
all, had been unforgivably insulted by the

wretched feline on a certain occasion in the past. For all her extreme circumspection, the Solemn Cow indulged in irony from time to time. Once, meeting the Cat in the farmyard where he had gone, no doubt, in the hope of stealing a little milk, she addressed him half-scornfully, half in jest, in a mixture of Portuguese and Spanish:

"*Chiquito*, you're much too little a fellow to be growing a moustache!"

The Cat had the unpardonable effrontery to answer back in kind:

"Lady, you're much too big a dame to be walking around without a bra!"

The Solemn Cow aimed a swift kick at him but the Cat sprang away, laughing his wicked laugh to himself. Everyone in the park thought the Cow had been terribly insulted. A number of families visited her that evening to try to comfort her, but she was inconsolable and couldn't stop crying.

First to call was the Reverend Parrot, who got tipsy later on and amused the company with entertaining anecdotes he had picked up in the seminary kitchen. Even the Solemn Cow stopped crying to laugh and finally she laughed so hard she was crying again.

When the Swallow told her how she had been amusing herself that afternoon, the Cow said she was only sorry the Swallow had not thrown rocks instead of twigs at the Cat's head while she was at it and done

47

away with him once and for all. When Missy looked horrified at such a blood-thirsty idea and then admitted that she had only thrown twigs at the Cat because she was looking for an excuse to strike up a conversation with him, it was the Cow's turn to be astonished.

"Conversation with the Cat? Are you really thinking, *loquita,* of conversing with the Cat? *Por Dios,* what folly!"

Speaking Spanish gave her status, but oh, how it tired her out! She went on in common Portuguese:

"Don't you know he's a cat, and a bad cat, and a young lady swallow can *never*— never, that is, if she cares for her family's honor and good name—have anything to do with cats? Don't you know that cats and swallows are sworn enemies, and that far too many of your female friends and relations have perished in the claws of cats like that one, striped or not?"

Once the Cow began preaching she never stopped. What did the foolish little swallow mean by breaking the old taboo, trampling on established custom and by so doing insulting her friends and breaking her parents' hearts?

"But he hasn't done me any harm—"

"He's a cat, isn't he? And a striped tom to boot!"

"But even if he *is* a striped tom cat, that doesn't mean he doesn't have a heart like the rest of us!"

"A heart?" cried the Solemn Cow indignantly (her indignation was easily aroused, as we are gradually finding out). "Whoever told you he had a heart? Who said so?"

"Well, I thought . . ."

"Have you ever seen his heart? Tell me that!"

"Why, no, I haven't seen it, exactly. . . ."

"Well then?"

She went on and on. The story of how the Cat had insulted her brought tears to her eyes as she told it, along with much more advice and dire warnings. Giving advice was a thing the Solemn Cow was very good at; she could rattle off all the rules of good conduct and morality, even if they were a little stuffy. She explained exactly how a young unmarried swallow should act and the things she must never, never do. The main thing she must never do was give the time of day to a cat, to a certain Striped Tom Cat in particular.

The Swallow listened politely because she had been well brought up, but her spirits drooped. No, she must not talk to the

Cat; it was wrong even to think about it. The Cow was more experienced and surely knew best, and that matron's lofty words and pear-shaped tones impressed her in spite of herself. And yet the stubborn little Swallow still could not understand what crime she would be committing by talking to the Cat. She promised the Cow all the same that she wouldn't throw twigs down on the Tom Cat's black and yellow back anymore and that she wouldn't even think of giving him the time of day.

But swallows' vows are light as air and no one should put too much faith in them, much less in the vows of an ardent young swallow with a spirit of adventure. In fact, I have a good notion Missy knew before the words were out of her mouth that she couldn't keep her promise. She continued to keep a close watch on the Cat just as before. She did stop throwing twigs at him, not because she had promised, I'm sorry to say, but because she was afraid he would think it was the Wind teasing him and go away. She went out looking for him every single day until Spring came into the park. . . .

And here my first chapter ends and we can go back and pick up where we had to leave off. Blame it on structural error or the promptings of modern literary wisdom, whichever you like.

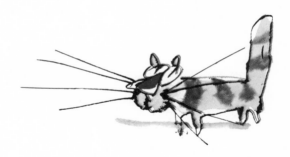

THE END OF
SPRING

Miss Swallow's parents scolded her good
and proper. But they were so overcome by
their own heroism—after all, they had
braved the Tom Cat to rescue their daughter—that they didn't scold her for very
long. Father Swallow said to Mother Swallow:

"We love our daughter so much we've
just saved her life."

"Yes," answered Mother Swallow, "see
what good parents we are! We take good
care of our daughter."

And they gazed at each other in mutual
admiration. After that they gave Miss Swallow strict instructions not to go near the
fierce enemy. If a young swallow's vows are
worth little, blunt prohibitions only shar-
pen her interest and natural curiosity. Not
that Missy was one of those swallows who
only need to be told not to do a thing for
her to immediately run off and do it. Not at
all; she was a gentle, obedient daughter
who loved her parents dearly, a kind, polite, well-behaved little swallow. But she
did think it was only fair for people to give
her a reason for what they told her to do or
not to do, and so far no one had used very
good arguments to persuade her that it was
a crime to be friendly with the Tom Cat.

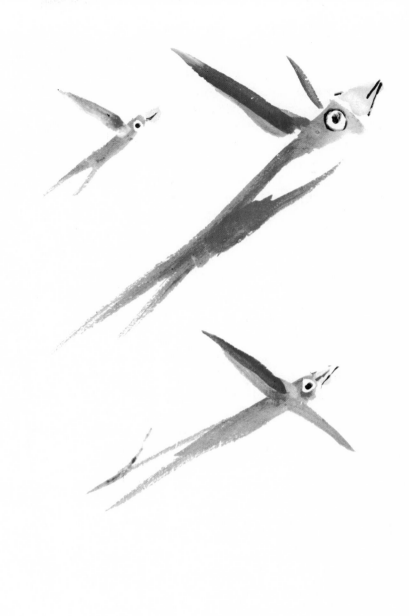

And so, when she laid her dear little head on her rose-petal pillow that night she had already made up her mind to seek out the Cat for a talk the next day.

"He's ugly, but he's nice," she whispered to herself as she dropped off to sleep.

As for the Striped Cat, he was thinking of none other than coy Miss Swallow that first night of Spring when he laid his head on his pillow—in a manner of speaking he did, for a pillow was one of the things he didn't have. Besides being wicked and ugly, Tom Cat was poor as Job and had to make do for a pillow by resting his head on his arms. Being unused to luxury he didn't complain. There were other things he missed more: love, affection, and Vienna sausages.

It was late when he went to bed. He had roamed aimlessly around the park all day long, scraping the bark off trees with his claws, meowing loudly for no good reason and feeling an almighty itch to prowl on the rooftops the way he used to do as a youngster. He sniffed the good smell of earth and his long whiskers stirred. He felt very young again, wished he could run with the dogs. And he would have done it, too, if the dumb dogs hadn't run off in a panic when he started after them. He felt such an ache of vague restlessness and yearning that he muttered to himself:

"I guess I'm sick." He placed his paw to his forehead. "I am burning with fever!"

When it was dark and he was on his way to bed—bed was an old scrap of velvet—he looked at a flower and saw the Swallow's big eyes in it. He stalked over to the pond for a drink to cool his fever and saw Missy's smiling reflection in the water. Then he started seeing her in every leaf, dewdrop, evening sunbeam and shadow of creeping dusk. Finally he spotted her all dressed in silver up in the full moon, to which he yowled a doleful serenade. The moon was high and far off by the time he got to sleep. He dreamed of the Swallow, the first time he had dreamed for so many years.

Should we jump to the conclusion that the Tom Cat, with his ugly dun-colored eyes and sinister reputation, has fallen in love? Now, while he and the Swallow are asleep and only Old Owl is awake, please bear with me while I philosophize a little. Philosophizing is a universally recognized right of all tellers of tales and I really ought to make use of it, if only to keep up the tradition. All I want to say is that some people don't believe in love at first sight, while others not only believe in it but swear it's the only kind of true love there is. Both are right. The truth is that love lies asleep in our hearts, ready to be awakened at the coming of Spring or the middle of Winter. It seems to happen more easily in Spring, but I needn't go into that here.

The point is that love can wake suddenly from its sleep at the sight of another. Even if we already know that other person, it's as if we saw him or her for the first time, and that's what we mean by love at first sight.

That's what the Tom Cat felt for Miss Swallow. As for what went on in Missy's brave little heart, don't expect me to reveal or explain it. I'm not so foolish as to think myself capable of understanding a woman's heart, much less a swallow's.

None of these thoughts occurred to the Striped Cat that night, needless to say. He didn't know he was in love; such a notion had not even entered his head. When he was young he used to fall in love every week, generally on Tuesdays, and out of love again by Friday, since he was a lazy cat and liked having Saturday, Sunday and Monday to rest up. He had broken the hearts of cats of all colors, and had even fallen for a gray rabbit and a tender young fox. But all that was so far in the past that he couldn't remember the circumstances or any of the ladies' names. These days he lived quietly in his corner, basking in the sun and enjoying the gentle caress of the breeze, the cool Summer nights and the sparkling cold Winter. And now Spring had come to ruin his peace of mind.

Next morning when he woke up and began washing his face with his paws, he thought of the Swallow and recalled the dream that had been with him all night— he and Missy arguing about who was pretty and who was ugly. "I must have had a touch of fever last night," he said to himself with a laugh. He stalked over to his favorite corner to sun himself on his old velvet rag while the life of the park went on around him.

So there was the Striped Cat, sprawled full length as usual so the Spring sun could wrap him around in its gentle warmth. Oddly enough, he could not seem to shut his eyes as he usually did. Experience had taught him that the warm sun and the cool breeze are even more delightful if you keep your eyes closed. On this second day of Spring, though, his eyes were open and turned toward the tree where Miss Swallow had perched the day before. When he realized what he was doing the Cat was furious. He stopped staring at the tree and turned away, whistling softly, to find something else to look at. He watched the dogs running and jumping—"That's all they know how to do, those idiots"—and the trees putting out leaves. And then, "Look, there's old Parrot pretending he's saying his morning prayers." The Parrot had one hand on his heart and his eyes were upturned to heaven. The Cat couldn't help sticking his tongue out at these unctuous, clerical airs. The Parrot, alarmed by the unexpected and threatening gesture, broke off his prayers for a conciliatory greeting.

"Why, bless me if it isn't old Tom Cat! Good morning, sir, and how's your health today? Quite well, I hope, the Lord be praised!"

The Cat did not trouble to answer. His gaze had already strayed back to the tree where the Swallow had perched the day before. While he stares at it, hoping to see her appear, I'll explain why he did such a

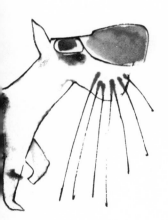

59

rude thing. It was not, as you might think, because the Tom Cat had no respect for religion. It was because he had no use for a hypocrite, and the Parrot was hypocrisy personified.

The Owl, who knew pretty well what sort of life each of her neighbors led, had once told the Cat that under all those religious pretentions Professor Parrot was nothing but a pious old fraud. He had made improper advances to the White Duckling, to the Speckled Hen, to a little turtledove he was catechizing and to cap it all, to the venerable Old Owl herself. And what about the Parrot Pigeon? There was a tale for you! One day Mrs. Carrier Pigeon gave birth to a mighty peculiar bird: a pigeon that spoke like a man. The male Pigeon, besides being rather a fool, was often away on long flights because he delivered all the letters in the park. Officially the baby pigeon was his child, but the Owl thought there was something funny about it. Who in that park besides the Parrot knew and spoke the language of men? The dogs understood it but they couldn't speak it. Besides, the Parrot was always running over to the Pigeon's house when her husband was away with the excuse of conveying "spiritual sustenance" to the little wife. Fortunately the Carrier Pigeon was a good-natured soul.

Tom Cat had nothing against a man with a roving eye. He never joined in the gossip about the way the Rooster carried on. That

dashing bird was enviably polygamous, a born Muhammadan who added another spring chicken to his well-stocked harem almost every day. All of the pigeons, who were confirmed monogamists, as well as the Black Duck, who was monogamous by default since there was only one female duck in the park, professed to be scandalized at the goings-on of that libertine Cock. The Solemn Cow shook her head in silent disapproval. The Cat was the only one who couldn't care less. He had nothing against libertines, but he couldn't stand hypocrites like the Parrot. That's why he stuck out his tongue at him in such a rude and insulting way.

I've been waiting and hoping all the time I've been telling you this that Miss Swallow would come and light on the tree in front of the Cat. But the ungrateful little minx hasn't shown up, and so we find our striped friend cross and down in the mouth, not at all the cheerful fellow we left a little while ago. The playful mood he was in when he got out of bed has quite vanished, and his long whiskers are drooping, dejected, limp. You can tell the Cat's spirits are low when his whiskers droop.

Once again he stared at the tree, as he had already done so many times before. Still no Swallow, and now the shadow of the tree fell across his big body. The dun-colored eyes grew dark. Why did his heart ache? And Spring buzzing and blooming all around him only made it worse.

Somehow he got up, he didn't know how or why—to get out of the shade and into the sun again, maybe. Anyhow he stood up and walked away. And before very long he noticed that his legs—maybe they knew better than he did where he wanted to go —had carried him all the way to the distant tree where the Swallow lived with her family, clear on the other side of the park.

Swallow's father and mother had gone out for food. The Swallow saw the Cat coming and waited for him with a smile. The Striped Cat stopped under the tree, peered all around and spotted Missy. Only then did he realize where he had got to without even knowing it. Blast it, he thought, what am I doing over here? Just as he had made up his mind to go back where he came from as fast as possible—Damn! his paws were so heavy they might as well have been made of lead—the Swallow chirped sweetly:

"Aren't you even going to say good morning, you rude thing?"

"Good morning, Missy," the Cat said not unmelodiously in his hollow voice.

"Miss Swallow, *if* you please."

Then, seeing his face fall (he was even homelier when he was sad), she relented.

"Oh, all right. You may call me Missy if it makes you happy. And I'll call you Ugly."

"I'm not ugly. I've already told you that."

"My, you're conceited! You're the ugliest person I ever saw. My godmother Owl would win a beauty prize next to you."

What was he doing there, anyway, the Tom Cat wondered. Instead of treating him with proper respect (but did he really want her to?), that little snip of a swallow insulted him, taunted him, and called him ugly. That was what came of humoring a young swallow who was nothing but a silly little schoolgirl, a pupil in old Parrot's religion class without a thought in her head. How could she hope to hold her own in conversation with a mature cat who had seen the world and was much more cultivated than any of the other folk in the park? And who, above all, considered himself an exceedingly handsome cat? He decided to go away and never say another word to the impertinent little bird (his feet felt as heavy as a ton of lead!). He got up to go. "Well, see you later. . . ."

"Oh, now I've gone too far and made him mad! He must be even more vain than he is ugly."

Now why the devil was he beginning to think this was funny? It wasn't just his feet that refused to obey him; his mouth opened in a broad grin just when he wanted to look stern and indignant. The whole world was conspiring to make a fool out of him. Miss Swallow chirped incessantly, an artless country girl whose radiant youth outshone everything around her.

"You don't have to go away, I won't call you ugly any more. From now on I'll call you beautiful."

"I don't want that either."

"What *shall* I call you, then?"

"Cat."

"Cat—I can't do that!"

"Why not?"

Was she unhappy all of a sudden? Her voice wasn't teasing any more. Tom Cat repeated his question.

"Why can't you?"

"I can't talk to a cat. Cats and swallows are enemies."

"Who told you that?"

"It's true. I just know it is."

Tom's face wore the saddest expression she had ever seen. The Swallow, who was naturally lighthearted and couldn't bear to see anyone else unhappy, hurried on.

"But *we* aren't enemies, are we?"

"Never!"

"Well, then it's all right for us to talk." But the next minute she added: "Go away, Father's coming! I'll fly over to the plum tree in a little while and we can talk there, my big old ugly Cat."

Tom Cat laughed and quickly disappeared into a bunch of the tall grass that grew all around, feeling cheerful again. As he bounded away through the brush he remembered his conversation with the Swallow and heard her tuneful voice echoing in his ears. So she couldn't talk to a cat. Cats were evil; cats had actually been caught lunching on swallows; there was some truth to that. How could any cat be so blackhearted as to gobble up a fragile, delicate little creature like Missy?

He lay down under the flowering plum tree and the Swallow soon joined him, turning circles in her flight and improvising a graceful Springtime ballet. The Nightingale, gazing at her from afar, began to sing until his exquisite love song filled the park.

The Cat clapped his paws when she alighted on a low branch. They took up their conversation where they had left off.

I won't write down everything they said anymore. All of their conversations were very much alike, and it was only little by little as time went on that they became worthy of a love story. Oh, well, maybe I'll set one down a little later when the time seems right. All I want to say for now is that they spent the whole Spring talking and never once ran out of things to say. They were getting acquainted, discovering new things about each other every day. They didn't only talk, of course. They wandered all over the park together, like inseparable friends, he running over the green grass, she flying through the blue sky. They explored everywhere, finding delightful corners and discovering new tints in the flowers, subtle variations in the gently blowing breeze, and a joy that came more from inside themselves than from what they saw and heard. Or perhaps the joy was part of everything around them and they hadn't realized it before. Because—and this I'm sure of—we have eyes for seeing and eyes for not seeing. Whether we see or not depends on the state of our hearts.

When they greeted each other in the morning, the Cat would ask:

"What have you been doing since yesterday, Missy? You're prettier today than you were yesterday, even prettier

than when I used to dream about you at night."

"All right, you tell me your dream. I won't tell you mine because I dreamed about someone very ugly—I dreamed of you!"

Then they would both laugh, he in his hollow wicked cat's guffaw, she in her silvery swallow's trill. And that's the story of what happened in Spring.

SUMMER

This won't be a very long chapter because Summer passed swiftly away with its burning sun and its nights full of stars. We all know how Time rushes by when we're happy. The truth is, Time never does what we want him to. When you beg him to linger awhile, he runs away as fast as he can and before you know it the happy days are gone. When you want him to fly away faster than a thought because you're unhappy or going through a bad time, you can't get rid of him and the hours creep by.

Summertime was brief for the Cat and the Swallow. They filled it with leisurely rambles, long talks under shady trees, smiles, murmurs, shy but expressive looks, and a tiff or two.

I don't know whether tiff is the right word. Let me explain. Sometimes the Swallow found the Cat looking downcast, with his whiskers drooping forlornly and his eyes dull brown instead of gold. The reason was always the same: he had seen the Swallow in the Nightingale's company, talking or singing—the Nightingale was her voice teacher. The Swallow could not understand the Striped Cat's sudden fits of melancholy, prolonged into awkward silences. Between her and the Cat not a word of love had been spoken, and, besides, she thought of the Nightingale as a brother, or so she said.

One day, a day when the voice lesson had gone on longer than usual and the Cat's whiskers drooped so low they touched the ground, she demanded to know why he was so unhappy and the Striped Cat told her.

"If I weren't a cat, I'd ask you to marry me."

The Swallow listened in silence as deep as a quiet Summer night. Was she surprised? I don't think so; she had guessed what had been happening in the Cat's heart. Was she angry? No, I don't think she was; his words made her heart leap up. But she was afraid. He was a cat, and cats and swallows will be enemies forever.

She flew low over Tom Cat, so low he could hear her little heart beating, and touched him lightly with her left wing. Then she flew up high into the sky and glanced back at him. It was the last day of Summer.

A Parenthetical Aside

FOR GOSSIP

(Whispered the Solemn Cow in the Parrot's ear: "Did you ever hear of such a thing? A swallow of the winged race keeping company with a cat of the feline race? Did you ever hear of such a thing in your life?" And the Parrot murmured in the ear of the Cow: "Our Father Who Art in Heaven, have you ever seen a swallow encouraging a cat? They do say, yes, they do, but I don't believe it, but maybe it's true, maybe it's true, that he wants to marry her, God Save and Preserve Me, well I do believe it, I do believe he does, Amen." And the male Carrier Pigeon cooed softly to the female: "Have you ever seen anything like it? A flighty young swallow running around with a cat? There's a law, an ancient law, that says pigeon mates with pigeon, duck with duck, bird with bird, dog with bitch, cat with cat. Whoever heard of a pretty little swallow taking a cat for her sweetheart?" And the female Pigeon cooed softly to her mate: "I don't know what things are coming to, it's the end of the world, there's no respect for law and order anymore." Whispered the Dog to the Bitch: "Poor little Swallow, enjoying the Cat's company so much, and all the time he's just waiting to pounce on her and gobble her up." The Bitch answered with a shake of her head: "Yes, that nasty Cat's just waiting to gobble her up." And the Duck said to his pretty Pepita: "I don't approve at all of that foolish Swallow's disgraceful carrying on. Her conduct is ugly, immoral, and rash. She talks to the Cat as if he

weren't a cat. And the Striped Cat of all cats, a born criminal!" Pepita the Duck agreed with her pompous mate. "Duck mates with duck, pigeon with pigeon, bitch with dog, hen with rooster, swallow with bird, and she-cat with he-cat." And the trees murmured as the Wind went by: "Who ever heard, who ever heard, who ever heard such a thing?" And flowers blushed and whispered in Earth's ear: "A Swallow can't marry, can't marry a Cat!" And they all sang in chorus: "It's a mortal sin!" Missy's father heard the rumors and so did her mother. Her father said angrily to her mother: "Our daughter's gone astray! Our daughter's taken up with the Striped Cat!" To which her mother replied: "Our daughter's a silly girl and it's high time she was married." "Yes," the father said, "but to whom?" "To the Nightingale," answered the mother. "He's already spoken to me about it." Now that was something the whole park approved of. "What a good marriage for the Swallow. The Nightingale is courtly and handsome and such a fine singer, and he belongs to the winged race. It's perfectly proper for Missy Swallow to marry him. The one she can't marry is the Striped Cat. Who in the world ever heard of a swallow mating with a cat?" "Three times Amen," said the Parrot.)

FALL

The next day Fall came blustering in, sweeping the leaves from the trees. The Wind felt cold and ran whistling through the park to take the chill out of his bones. Fall brought a trail of clouds to paint the sky gray. It wasn't only the scenery that had changed with the seasons as my perceptive readers have surely noticed by now. The park's attitude toward the Striped Tom Cat had undergone a marked change. Not that his neighbors didn't still bear a grudge against him, not that they had forgiven him for his old sins. It was just that they were no longer afraid of him, as the gossip about his love affair with the Swallow plainly shows. Fearful whispers had swollen to a loud, buzzing rumor. My readers will recall that not so long ago, in the first few pages of this book, the park's residents would all quake in their boots if the Tom Cat batted an eye at them. How to explain, then, that they weren't afraid of him any longer and dared to gossip freely, almost openly, about his romance with Miss Swallow?

It was because the Cat had been so contented and happy all that Spring and Summer. He had not bullied a living soul, had not kicked a single flower, had not made the hair on his back stand up when strangers approached, or bristled and spat insults between his teeth to keep the dogs at bay. He had turned into a gentle, good-natured creature who was the first to say "hello" when he met a fellow inhabitant of the park; he, the Cat who used to ignore the fearful "good mornings" of the others.

I would even venture to say that the Cat nurtured kind and generous sentiments at that time. And I base this rash statement on the fact, among other less important signs, that he risked his life to drive out the Rattlesnake when she sneaked into the park that Summer. Everybody else hid when they saw her, even the Great Dane puppy who always growled threateningly when a stranger came around.

The Cat ran straight up to the Rattlesnake, dodged nimbly away from her mortal thrust, and rained so many blows on her head that she glided off as fast and as far as she could and never came back to the park again.

The Swallow was the only one to praise the Cat's feat. All the others thought he had only stood up to the Rattler to cut a fine figure and look brave. The Solemn Cow even professed to be sorry that the Snake's forked tongue had missed. The Parrot called it "blatant exhibitionism."

The truth was that the Striped Cat had a reputation to live down as a wicked, unsociable fellow. Seeing him so very affable, the park's inhabitants had concluded that, although he might still be very wicked, he was no longer much of a threat. He was probably growing feeble and trying to reform in his old age. Soon their fear of him was gone. The Parrot began to cultivate the Cat's society out of self-interest, in the hope of gaining his friendship and using him somehow against his, the Parrot's, enemies; the Duck, for instance, who said terrible things about him behind his back. The Cat tolerated the Parrot's presence (the old fraud was a link with his Swallow in a way, since he taught her religion) but discouraged any attempt at familiarity. The Parrot was so offended at the snub that he spread a cruel theory to explain the Cat's unusual gentleness: the cause of his changed behavior was an incurable disease. Finding himself at death's door, the Cat was seeking forgiveness for his sins.

This sort of nonsense should not be taken as proof of universal spitefulness in the community. The Tom Cat's evil reputation was of very long standing, after all. How could his neighbors be expected to understand that the Cat had changed since the Swallow entered his life? How could they know that beneath the bristling hair of a tough Tom Cat beat a tender heart?

Such a tender heart that the first day of Autumn found the Striped Cat hard at work on a sonnet. With a heavy wool blanket thrown over him (the Cat was highly susceptible to cold), he was counting syllables on his fingers and searching for rhymes in a fat dictionary edited by Professor Anteater, a famous lexicographer, literary prizewinner and member of the Academy of Letters. Yes, the Striped Cat actually produced a sonnet. I have in my possession a copy of this sole literary production of the no-nonsense cat who had never dreamed of indulging in such flights of fancy before. It was given to me by Dr. Cururu, the Toad—who turns his hand to literary criticism when he has nothing better to do—as a horrible example of a botched lyric poem. He is certainly right about that. What's more, the illustrious Toad discovered a monstrous plagiarism in the Cat's brief literary effort, and no one would care to contradict a pronouncement backed by the incontestable authority of Dr. Cururu Toad.

So that the reader may judge the sonnet for himself and decide whether the accusations of plagiarism are true or false, I reproduce the verses in question below verbatim. I can't plunk them right in the middle of my story; this is not a book of poetry, after all—much less a book of bad, plagiarized sonnets—but a tale the Wind told Morning and Morning told Time, to win a blue rose. I'll just have to slip in another parenthetical aside, a poetic one this time.

I ask of the reader only one thing: that when judging the Cat's sonnet he remember the good intentions with which the amateur bard touched his lyre and indulgently overlook his lack of literary vocation and talent. On that morning of lyric inspiration the Tom Cat wrapped himself not merely in a blanket but in a mantle of love. Poetry is found in a lover's heart as well as in his verse, and sometimes that love is too great to fit into words.

A Parenthetical Poem

A LOVELORN SONNET FOR MY
ADORED MISS SWALLOW BY TOM CAT

Missy my Swallow
Missy my Dove
Flew up to Heaven
And took my love.

Life ain't worth living
Can't sing, can't fly
Got no wings, got no feathers
And my poems make me cry.

Love my Swallow so
Wish she'd marry me, oh!
But she won't have me, no!

She can't marry me
I'm a cat, you see,
And woe is me.

by Tom Cat

POSTSCRIPT

In order to give the reader a solid basis on which to form his own confident judgment I offer another parenthetical aside, a critical one this time. The reader may wonder why this story is interrupted so often with parenthetical asides while the author takes his ease, snoring in a hammock, no doubt, or playing around; but actually it's the reader who comes out ahead. Instead of wasting his time over a foolish love story he can gain valuable insights from the serious essay that follows. It comes from the pen of none other than the eminent Dr. Cururu Toad, a member of both the Academy and the Institute, literary critic and professor of communications. Without further ado I yield the floor to the Master.

Parenthetical Criticism

CONTRIBUTED AT THE REQUEST OF THE AUTHOR BY
DR. CURURU TOAD, MEMBER, LITERARY INSTITUTE

(This poor attempt at a poem lacks any profound idea and suffers from innumerable defects of form. The language lacks fluency; its grammatical structure does not obey the canons laid down by the sublime poets of the past; the poet rides roughshod over the meter, where strictness ought to be the rule; the rhyme scheme, which should be sumptuous, is threadbare when it deigns to appear at all.

Most unpardonable of all, however, is the blatant crime committed in the first quatrain of the sonnet allegedly composed by the Striped Cat: an obvious plagiarism of a vulgar carnival song that goes as follows:

> 'Yayá the cockroach
> Yoyô the roach
> Flew up to Heaven
> In a golden coach.'

The plagiarist and poetaster whom I have dragged before the bar of public opinion in order to expose him for the thief he is—the more reprobate he since it is only ideas he steals—not content with his crime, chose to copy low doggerel howled out by the mob in the streets. If the strength of his intellect was too feeble to conceive an original poetic work of any merit, could he not at least have plundered one of the great masters—Homer, Dante, Vergil, Milton, or Basílio de Magalhães?

CURURU TOAD, PH.D.)

FALL

Now that the Tom Cat's sonnet has been criticized, dissected and found wanting, we can get back to our story. That is, we can get on with the sonnet. That sonnet wasn't dragged in just to fill up space, you know; it has a great deal to do with all that comes next.

The last day of Summer was the beginning of the end. After that last scene between the Swallow and the Cat, the Cat had a long talk with the Owl. Of all the creatures in the park the Owl was the only one who appreciated the Cat, as we have already seen. The Swallow had not returned after what had happened that evening. The Cat tried to understand what was passing through her mind and what conflicting emotions she must be a prey to. Feeling sad and forsaken himself, he went off to take counsel with the Owl, who was just waking up from her old woman's sleep and opening her eyes to greet her dear friend, Night.

The Cat sat down beside Owl on the branch of a Jack Tree, and at first they talked about unimportant things. But the Owl was a diviner, and she guessed what

87

had brought the Striped One to see her. She was open with him; she repeated the malicious talk that was making the rounds of the park, which naturally enraged the Cat, and in the end she told him honestly what she thought.

"There's nothing you can do, old friend. How could you ever have thought the Swallow would have you for a husband? There was never any hope of that. Even if she loved you—and who's to say she does?—she could never marry you. Swallows have been forbidden to marry cats since the beginning of time. And that prohibition is more than just a law, it's an instinct planted deep in every swallow's heart. You say she loves you, that if she could have her own way . . . well, maybe so. Yes, I think you may be right. But the law of the swallows is stronger than she is. That's because it's been inside her since her great-great-grandmother's time, ever since the very first swallow was made. And it takes a revolution to break a law like that."

Shaking her head, she added, "Not that a little revolution wouldn't be a good idea. I think we need one."

The Cat said nothing at all. It was no use loving Miss Swallow, no use dreaming of lying beside her on a torn scrap of velvet. He had forgotten that swallows sleep in nests in the treetops, while cats sleep on old rags on the ground. He took his leave of the

Owl without any outward sign that he would heed her advice. As soon as he got home he began writing the famous sonnet. It took him all that night and part of the next morning to finish it, and all he was able to achieve was the effort we have already judged and condemned.

Later that first day of Fall he met the Swallow. She was grave and unsmiling, without the blithe air of being ready for a frolic which was her greatest charm. The Cat couldn't hide his own unhappiness either; the Owl's words weighed like a stone on his heart. They walked and flew in silence through all the places they had visited in Spring and Summer. Once in a while they exchanged a word or two, but it was plain they were both avoiding a subject that couldn't be put off for long.

It was time for the Swallow to go. The Cat handed her his sonnet and she flew away, turning her dear head every so often to look back at him. There were tears in her eyes.

The next day—oh, it was the longest day of Autumn—she did not appear at all. Tom Cat prowled in vain around the tree where she lived; she was nowhere to be seen. That night he remembered and resented the park's malicious gossip. He chased the Black Duck, frightened the Parrot at his evening prayers, clawed the Great Dane's muzzle, robbed some eggs from the

chicken coop and, worst crime of all, didn't eat them but threw them away in a field. Fear of the Tom Cat lurked in the park again and the buzzing gossip died down to a furtive whisper.

On the third day of Fall the Carrier Pigeon threw down a letter from a safe distance. Tom Cat read it over so many times he soon learned it by heart. It was a sad but firm letter from Miss Swallow. "A swallow can never marry a cat," it said, and added that they mustn't see each other anymore.

90

To soften the blow, she had also written that the only times she had ever been really and truly happy were when she was exploring the park with the Striped Cat. And she closed with "Ever yours, Missy."

She had promised not to see him anymore. But as I said before and now say again, a swallow's word can't be trusted. They roamed through the park again and went to all the favorite hidden places they had discovered in Spring. The only difference was that now they hardly spoke, as if an invisible curtain hung between them.

They spent most of Fall that way, in gray weather, as the trees shed their leaves one by one and the sky shed its blue. Since the Striped Cat was feared as before and lived apart like a hermit, talking to no one, he did

not know that six spider seamstresses were in Miss Swallow's house, sewing the young bride's trousseau. The date for the wedding of the Nightingale and Miss Swallow was set for the beginning of Winter.

On the last day of Fall, a damp, misty day scoured by a wind that shuddered with cold, the Swallow said she wanted to revisit all the places they had learned to love in Summer and Spring. She was strangely wild and talkative that day, as loving and full of flirtatious charm as though the distance that had opened between them had shrunk to nothing again. She was the old Swallow of Spring and Summer, a little flighty and rambunctious, and the Tom Cat was touched.

They roamed together all day until nightfall. Then she told him that that day had been their last, that she was going to marry the Nightingale because, oh!, because a Swallow can't marry a Cat. Just as she had done on a certain other day, she skimmed low over his head and flicked him lightly with her left wing—it was her way of giving him a kiss—but this time he could not hear her little heart beat at all, so feebly did it throb. Then she flew up into the sky and left him without looking back.

WINTER

I should make this a long chapter because
the first days of Winter were a weary time
of pain. But why talk about such sad things,
why dwell on the dreadful deeds of the
Tom Cat, whose eyes were now so dark
they looked black? The letters written in
the park and sent via the Carrier Pigeon to
other parks told all about them. The news
reached the far-off lair of the Diamondback
Rattler and even she trembled with fear.
The Cat's wickedness was a favorite subject, but so, too, was his loneliness. The
Striped Cat never spoke to anyone these
days. His terrible solitude touched the
heart of a Tea Rose who confided to her
new lover the Jasmine Vine:

"Poor thing! Living all by himself like
that, without anyone or anything in the
world to call his own."

The Tea Rose was mistaken in thinking
that the Striped Cat lived bereft and alone.
He owned a whole world full of memories,
of lovely moments relived and happy recol-
lections. I'm not saying he was happy or
that he didn't suffer. He suffered very
much, but he did not despair; he still drew
nourishment from what he had been given.
But the sadness never left him. Happiness
needs more than memories of the past to

93

feed on; it also needs dreams of the future.

Swallow's wedding with the Nightingale took place on a day of pale Winter sun. There were great festivities and a long table with sweets and champagne. The civil marriage was held at the bride's house; the Rooster was Judge and made an eloquent speech about the duties of a virtuous wife, especially that of being faithful to her husband. Of a husband's duty to be faithful to his wife he said nothing. He was a Muhammadan, not a hypocrite; everyone knew that Don Juan of Rhode Island kept a harem. The couple exchanged their religious vows in the orange tree, the pretty chapel of the park. The Reverend Father Vulture came from a distant monastery to preside over the religious ceremony, and the Parrot served as sacristan and got very drunk that night. The Vulture's sermon was very moving and Swallow's mother cried a lot.

As the nuptial procession fluttered out of the chapel, Swallow caught sight of Tom Cat off to one side. She contrived to fly directly over him and drop a petal from a red rose in her bridal bouquet. The Cat placed it over his heart, where it looked like a drop of blood.

If I wanted this story to have a happy ending I'd have to describe the reception given that night by the parents of the bride, perhaps even tell my readers a few of the anecdotes the Parrot recited to amuse the guests. Everyone who lived in the park was

94

there except the Striped Cat. Morning described the festivities to Time, complete with minute details of the gowns, the refreshments, the delicious cakes, and the decoration of the room.

But all of this the reader can perfectly well imagine his own way. I only want to say that the orchestra of birds played exquisitely and that its dulcet strains floated out to where the Striped Cat crouched alone in the park. There was no longer any future in which to sustain his impossible dream of love. The night of Miss Swallow's wedding feast was a night without stars. All that was left for him was the red rose petal over his heart like a drop of blood.

NIGHT
WITHOUT STARS

The music made his heart ache. The nuptial song of the bride and groom was a funeral chant to the Tom Cat. He took his rose petal, looked around one last time at the park sheathed in Winter, and walked slowly away. He knew a place a long way off where nobody lived but the Rattlesnake, who avoided the parks and planted fields where she was unwelcome. The Cat headed for that deserted place along narrow roads that lead to the crossroads at the end of the world.

He passed in front of the festive house just in time to see the bride and the bridegroom leaving. The Swallow saw him, too, and guessed where he was going, and something rolled down from the sky onto the petal the Cat was holding in his paw. On the blood-red rose petal gleamed a Swallow's tear to light the solitary footsteps of the Striped Cat on a starless night.

And so we come to the end of the story that Morning heard from the Wind and told to Time, who gave her the blue rose he had promised. On certain Spring days Morning wears that legendary rose on her dress made of light, and we say it's a glorious, sky-blue day.

AMEN (said the Parrot)

Paris, November 1948